Nomit AND Pickle
go camping

C. E. Cameron

Clink
Street

Published by Clink Street Publishing 2021

Copyright © 2021

First edition.

ISBNs:
978-1-913962-47-0 paperback
978-1-913962-48-7 ebook

For Lucy

Daughter, sister, mother, wife, friend forever.

1975 - 2019

X

Pickle was bored one day and didn't know what to do.

As usual, she had been riding her bike and ringing her bell as loudly as possible in order to get her brother's attention.

Nomit however, was busy as he had plans today in other parts of Bellaland.

"What are you doing Nomit?" said Pickle, as she realised her brother was doing something that looked far more interesting than she could ever imagine.

"I'm going to go camping," said Nomit and then added, "on my own!" Both Nomit and Pickle knew that Bellaland was full of amazing places to go camping, although Pickle had never actually been allowed to go before.

"Oh please let me come along," pleaded Pickle. "I'll be good and pack all my own things."

"Very well," agreed Nomit, "but we leave in an hour so don't be late as usual!"

Nomit was extremely apprehensive about bringing his little sister along as his well organised plans usually went astray when Pickle was allowed to be involved.

"Are you ready yet?"

"Nearly!" said Pickle.

"Are you sure you've got everything?"

"Yes," said Pickle.

"Off we go then!"

Nomit had his rucksack packed, his map in hand and his route planned for a great walk through the woods to a lakeside location that he had spotted before.

Pickle however, was as usual less than organised with many items about to fall out of her bag.

Once in the woods it became clear that Pickle had chosen the wrong shoes to wear.

"My flippers and snorkel are difficult to walk in through the woods!" she complained.

An exasperated Nomit was not surprised by her poor choice of footwear.

They finally arrived at the lake, which was sparkling blue with pine trees all around.

They started setting up their tents, Nomit methodically referring to the instructions while Pickle upended the entire contents of her rucksack on the forest floor to see what she had brought with her.

Thirty minutes later, Nomit's tent was up and his belongings neatly organised inside. He was now very excited about their dinner and as usual had brought more food than he probably needed.

Pickle, however, had turned her tent inside out and was struggling to secure it as she had forgotten her tent pegs. Nomit had no patience at his sister's lack of organisation as he had seen it all before. He was far more excited about cooking the food that he had brought. Sausages, bacon and eggs, which were his favourites!

He placed them out ready to be cooked while Pickle continued to erect her tent-like structure.

"Please can you help me?" said Pickle.

But Nomit simply pointed out that she had wanted to come along and that, once again, she had failed to be organised.

It was only then that Nomit had a sudden hollow feeling in his stomach. He had been so excited about what he was packing for his dinner that he had forgotten his stove.

He then, however, realised that his sister had left one lying around in the dust.

Pickle agreed to let Nomit use her stove if he helped her put up her tent. Nomit set up her tent and then the two of them sat down to cook Nomit's food as Pickle had also forgotten to pack any for herself.

It didn't matter though as Nomit had packed more than enough food supplies for both of them.

They cooked their food and while enjoying it by the lake agreed that they would learn from their latest adventure.

Nomit & Pickle's – "Thought for the Day"

So, what had Nomit & Pickle learnt from their day out camping?

That "sharing is caring".

Nomit and Pickle now look forward to their next adventure...

Lightning Source UK Ltd.
Milton Keynes UK
UKHW050654030321
379663UK00003B/20